S E R I E S

Who Am I With Others?

Group

Loveland, Colorado

Christian Character Development Series: Who Am I With Others?

Visit our Web site: **www.grouppublishing.com**

Credits

Contributing Authors: Tim Baker, Stacy L. Haverstock, Mikal Keefer, Jan Kershner, and Paul Woods
Editor: Julie Meiklejohn
Creative Development Editor: Karl Leuthauser
Chief Creative Officer: Joani Schultz
Copy Editor: Betty Taylor
Art Director: Kari K. Monson
Cover Art Director: Jeff A. Storm
Cover Designer and Artist: Alan Furst, Inc. Art and Design
Computer Graphic Artist: Pat Miller
Illustrator: Amy Bryant
Production Manager: Peggy Naylor

ISBN 0-7644-2127-1
Printed in the United States of America.
10 9 8 7 6 5 4 3 2 1   01 00 99

Contents

*God wants us to **know** him.*

Christ shows us the best way to handle conflict.

Because God has forgiven us, we can forgive others.

God shows us how to be good friends to one another.

Human authority is given by God.

The Bible gives us solid guidelines for good dating relationships.

God's constant presence gives us comfort and hope in lonely times.

We are to follow Christ's example of love.

Introduction

Our teenagers may be talking the talk, but are they walking the walk? Often an enormous gap exists between the Christian values many teenagers claim to have and their actions. Take a moment to ponder these sobering statistics:

• Six out of ten Christian teenagers say there is no such thing as absolute truth.

• One out of four denies the notion that acting in disobedience to God's laws brings about negative consequences.

• One-half believe the main purpose of life is enjoyment and personal fulfillment.

• Almost half contend that sometimes lying is necessary.

What's wrong with this picture?

Today's teenagers face more choices than any teenagers before them have. They must interpret, evaluate, and make moral decisions within a culture that ignores morality and changes rapidly. The choices your teenagers make today have eternal consequences. Can their faith keep up?

How can we help? We can begin by taking them on a journey—a journey toward stronger, more Christlike character. As teenagers learn to interpret and evaluate their decisions in light of their relationships with God, they will discover the importance of living out their faith in everything they do.

How to Use This Book

Who Am I With Others? contains eight studies, each designed to address a different type of relationship or relationship issue teenagers encounter.

• The study about **knowing God** will help students understand the difference between knowing about God and truly knowing him, as well as helping them develop strategies to develop a more intimate relationship with God.

• The study about **conflict** will help teenagers see that Christ offers them the best way to handle conflict in their lives.

- The **forgiveness** study helps students understand the reason for forgiving others and themselves, as well as encouraging them to begin the hard work of forgiveness.

- The study about **friendship** will show teenagers how to build and maintain God-centered friendships.

- The study about **parents and other authorities** gives students tools for working with the authority figures in their lives, rather than battling against them.

- The **dating** study helps teenagers keep Christ at the center of their dating relationships.

- The study about **loneliness** will help students realize that God is always with them, even during their loneliest times.

- The study about **love** will encourage students to follow Christ's example of love in every aspect of their lives.

The Christian Character Development Series encourages students to examine their own character in a very individual, personal way. Each study in this series guides students to examine the topic individually, in pairs, and in larger groups.

Each study connects the topic and the Scriptures to God-centered character development—the idea that God gives us a model of quality character in his Word, as well as a desire to know him and to become more like him.

Each person in your group (including you) will have his or her own book to use extensively throughout each study for journaling and other writing and drawing activities. Each study begins with a section called "Read About It" and then follows with a section called "Write About It." These sections provide teenagers with "food for thought" about the topic and provide the opportunity to respond to those thoughts, right in their books. You may choose to have your students complete these sections before your group meets, or you may decide to have students complete these sections at the beginning of your meeting time.

Other sections of the book are designed so students can work through them with a minimum of direction from you. Any direction you may need to give your students is included in the "Leaders Instructions" boxes. You're encouraged to participate and learn right along with the students—your insights will enhance students' learning.

Each study provides a combination of introspective, active, and interactive learning. Teenagers learn best by experiencing the topic they're learning about and then sharing their thoughts and reactions with others.

The Christian Character Development Series will help you guide your teenagers through the perils and pitfalls of growing up in today's culture. Use the studies in this book to work with your youth to understand what it means to have high standards of character and to learn why character is important to God.

Other Topics

Who Am I When Nobody's Looking?

Honesty

Wisdom

Trust

Humility

Compassion

Generosity

Integrity

Faithfulness

Who Am I to God?

Salvation

The Bible

The Trinity

Prayer

Service

Faith

Sharing Faith

Worship

Who Am I...Really?

Righteousness

Popularity

Success

Self-Esteem

The Family of God

Spiritual Gifts

Role Models and Heroes

Dreams of the Future

Who Am I Inside?

Anger

Peace

Pride

Grief

Joy

Guilt

Fear

Hope

Who Am I to Judge?

Sex

Drugs and Alcohol

Peer Pressure

Moral Absolutes

Idolatry

Media and Music

Handling Stress

Making Good Decisions

Getting to Know God

 **God wants us to *know* him.**

Supplies: You'll need Bibles, pencils or pens, poster board, markers, modeling clay, various art supplies, and skit props such as old hats and glasses.

Preparation: On a table, set out the supplies to use during the study.

Leader Instructions

Begin by having students each read the "Read About It" section and respond in the "Write About It" section.

Read About It

All of God's revealed truths are sealed until they are opened to us through obedience. You will never open them through philosophy or thinking. But once you obey, a flash of light comes immediately...The only way you can get to know the truth of God is to stop trying to find out and by being born again. If you obey God in the first thing he shows you, then he instantly opens up the next truth to you. You could read volumes on the work of the Holy Spirit, when five minutes of total, uncompromising obedience would make things as clear as sunlight...It is not study that brings understanding to you, but obedience. Even the smallest bit of obedience opens heaven, and the deepest truths of God immediately become yours. Yet God will never reveal more truth about himself to you, until you have obeyed what you know already.

(Oswald Chambers, *My Utmost for His Highest*)

Write About It

• According to this reading, how do we get to know God? Do you agree? Why or why not?

_____

_____

_____

_____

- How well do you feel you know God right now? Do you just know *about* him, or do you know him *personally?* Explain.

_____

_____

- How does your life reflect your knowledge of God?

_____

_____

- Read 1 Corinthians 2:9-16. According to this passage, how can you really know God?

_____

_____

_____

- Why do you think God wants us to know him?

_____

_____

_____

Experience It

Find a partner (preferably someone you don't know well). Answer this question about your partner:

- What do you know about this person? List several things.

_____

_____

Now interview your partner using the following questions:

- What is your full name?

_____

- What was your favorite toy when you were little?

_____

- What do you want to do after you graduate from high school?

_____

Tell Me More...

"[True friendship with God] means being so intimately in touch with God that you never even need to ask him to show you his will. It is evidence of a level of intimacy which confirms that you are nearing the final stage of your discipline in the life of faith. When you have a right-standing relationship with God, you have a life of freedom, liberty, and delight; you *are* God's will. And all of your commonsense decisions are actually his will for you, unless you sense a feeling of restraint brought on by a check in your spirit. You are free to make decisions in the light of a perfect and delightful friendship with God, knowing that if your decisions are wrong he will lovingly produce that sense of restraint."

(Oswald Chambers, *My Utmost for His Highest*)

• What are your favorite things to do in your free time?

Now answer these questions on your own:

• Based on the information you had before and the information you just gained, do you think you really *know* your partner? Explain.

• What would it take for you to feel as if you really knew your partner?

Leader Instructions

When students have finished processing their interviews, have a few volunteers share their answers to the questions with the whole group. Then have students form new groups of three or four.

In your group, brainstorm answers to this question, and write your thoughts in the space provided.

• What do you know about God?

In your group, read Acts 17:24-31. Discuss the following questions, and jot down your thoughts.

• Did you discover anything about God that wasn't already on your list? If so, write those things here:

_____

_____

_____

_____

• Based on your thoughts and the knowledge in this Scripture passage, do you feel you *know* God? Why or why not?

_____

_____

• How is knowing about God similar to knowing about your partner? How is it different?

_____

_____

• How is *knowing* God different from *knowing about* God?

_____

_____

_____

• What would it take for you to feel as if you really knew God? Do you think it's possible to really know God?

_____

_____

_____

Leader Instructions

Have groups report their observations to the whole class. Then direct students to begin the next part of the study on their own.

On the graph below, chart your growth in knowing God throughout your life.

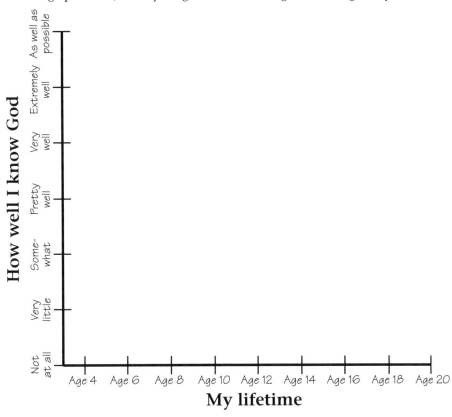

Once you've completed the graph, get together with your original partner and compare graphs. Discuss these questions:

• Based on your graph, how well do you feel you know God right now?

_____

_____

_____

• Why is it important to know God?

_____

_____

_____

Apply It

With your partner, brainstorm as many answers as you can think of to the following question, and then write your thoughts in the space provided:

Develop a profile of someone who knows God. Lay a long sheet of newsprint on the floor, have someone lie down on it, and trace around that person's body. Then hang the outline on the wall. On appropriate areas of the outline, have students fill in thoughts to develop the profile. For example, near the heart, a student might write, "Loves to spend time with God."

• How can we better know God?

_____

_____

The book of Psalms is a journal of sorts, chronicling a human attempt to more intimately know God. With your partner, divide these passages from Psalms (each partner will take three), and read them on your own. As you read, think about what each passage says about ways to know God better. Write your thoughts in the space next to each passage:

• Psalm 5:7 _____
• Psalm 7:1-2 _____
• Psalm 9:1-2 _____
• Psalm 19:7-11 _____
• Psalm 27:7-8 _____
• Psalm 27:14 _____

Share your responses with your partner. Then using the information you've gathered and the supplies provided, work together to create something that represents ways to know God better. For example, you might want to create a reading that incorporates parts of the psalms you just read, or you might want to draw, sculpt, or act out something that demonstrates building a closer relationship with God.

Leader Instructions 🖊

Allow pairs at least ten minutes to create their representations. Then have pairs each share their creations with the whole class.

Direct students to begin the next part of the study on their own.

Answer these questions:

• After today's study, I feel I know God (check one):

Much better _____

A little better _____

About the same _____

• As you get to know God better, how do you think your life will change? How will this change be reflected every day in your actions?

_____

_____

_____

• What will you do in the coming weeks to get to know God better?

_____

_____

_____

• Write the name of someone you will tell about your commitment and who will keep you accountable as you strive to get to know God better.

_____

_____

_____

One great way to know God better is by spending time in conversation with him. Spend a few minutes praying (either silently or aloud) for your partner, asking God to help him or her continue to seek to know God better.

Live It

Work on this section this week. You may sit down and do it all at once or work on it a little bit each day for several days. Try to establish a pattern of regularly meeting with God, and journal your thoughts each time you do.

Tell Me More...

For a serious look at what it means to know God and a challenge to do so, check out *Knowing God* by J. I. Packer. It won't be a light read, but if you're serious about making the most of your relationship with God, it is well worth the effort.

• Read Philippians 4:6-7. Write the elements of prayer according to this passage. Journal your thoughts about how such prayers might contribute to knowing God. Then pray, using the ideas in this passage.

_____

_____

_____

• Read 2 Corinthians 10:3-5. What do you think this passage has to do with getting to know God? Journal your thoughts as you think about what this passage means in your life. Then spend time in prayer, asking God to help you "take captive every thought to make it obedient to Christ."

_____

_____

_____

• Read 2 Timothy 2:15. Think about each phrase of the verse, one phrase at a time. According to this verse, determine what you think God might want you to do. Journal your thoughts. In order to help you learn more about the "word of truth," develop a plan for reading God's Word regularly, perhaps beginning with Mark—the simplest presentation of God in Jesus.

_____

_____

_____

• Read 1 John 4:7-12. Think about what loving others has to do with knowing God. Journal your thoughts about how your actions reflect your knowledge of God. Spend time in prayer, and then live out your prayer by doing something to demonstrate God's love working through you.

_____

_____

_____

_____

Conquering Conflict

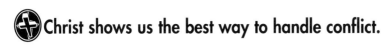 Christ shows us the best way to handle conflict.

Supplies: You'll need Bibles, pens or pencils, and markers and colored pencils.

Preparation: On a table, set out the supplies to use during the study.

Leader Instructions

Begin by having students each read the "Read About It" section and respond in the "Write About It" section.

Read About It

Don't wash their feet, Jesus. Tell them to wash yours.

That's what we want to say. Why? Because of the injustice? Because we don't want to see our King behaving as a servant?...

Or do we object because we don't want to do the same?...

Logic says: "Put up your fists."

Jesus says: "Fill up the basin."

Logic says: "Bloody his nose."

Jesus says: "Wash his feet."

Logic says: "She doesn't deserve it."

Jesus says: "You're right, but you don't, either."

...John 13:12 says, "When he had finished washing their feet..."

Please note, he *finished* washing their feet. That means he left no one out...That also means he washed the feet of Judas.

That's not to say it was easy for Jesus.

That's not to say it is easy for you.

That is to say that God will never call you to do what he hasn't already done.

(Max Lucado, *A Gentle Thunder*)

Write About It

• How do you think this reading might apply to conflicts you experience?

_____

_____

_____

• What's the biggest source of conflict in your life right now?

_____

_____

_____

_____

• What do you do when someone makes you angry?

_____

_____

_____

_____

• What do you think are the three best ways to handle conflict with another person? How often do you follow your own advice?

_____

_____

_____

_____

Experience It

Leader Instructions

Have students form four groups, and point out the supply table you've prepared before class.

In your group, follow the instructions and complete all the sections on the "The Good, the Bad, and the Ugly—How to Handle Conflict" page (p. 17). Use the supplies on the supply table as needed.

Tell Me More...

"If we could read the secret history of our enemies, we should find in each man's life sorrow and suffering enough to disarm all hostility."

—Henry Wadsworth Longfellow

The Good, the Bad, and the Ugly
How to Handle Conflict

Section 1

Read Luke 6:27-28. In your group, discuss the following questions. Write your answers in the space provided.

• Have you ever been around someone you knew hated you? How did you respond?

_____

_____

• On a scale of one to ten (ten is high), how difficult do you think it is to love someone who hates you? Why do you think Jesus would ask this of you?

_____

_____

• What's your first reaction when someone curses you or mistreats you?

_____

_____

Choose two people in your group to pantomime an argument. Have the two actors move away from the group for a minute to discuss what kind of argument they'll act out. Then have them come back and present their pantomime.

After the performance, discuss these questions and write the answers in the space provided.

• How realistic was the situation the actors depicted?

_____

_____

• Did the actors follow the advice of the Scripture you just read? What could they have done differently to follow that advice?

_____

_____

Now have two other members of your group act out the same situation, this time following the advice of the Bible passage.

Section 2

Read Luke 6:29-31. As a group, think of a scenario to depict one of the situations in the Scripture. For example, you might think of a fight starting outside school or a man begging on the street. Then use the art supplies provided to create your own four-frame cartoon on the next page, showing the scenario played out by following the advice of the Scripture. In each frame of the cartoon, write thought balloons for your characters.

After you've finished drawing and writing, present and explain your cartoon to the other members of your group.

<table>
<tr><td></td><td></td><td></td><td></td></tr>
<tr><td></td><td></td><td></td><td></td></tr>
</table>

Section 3

Read Luke 6:32-34. As a group, discuss the following questions and write your answers in the space provided.

• Who are the "sinners" Jesus refers to in these verses?

_____

_____

• Have you ever been one of those "sinners"? Describe the situation.

_____

_____

• Brainstorm common sayings in our society that express the opposite viewpoint from the one expressed in this Scripture. A few examples are "Nice guys finish last" and "Look out for number one!" List as many sayings as you can think of.

_____

_____

Section 4

Read Luke 6:35-36. Answer the following questions. Then share your answers with the rest of the group.

• We know we can't *earn* eternal life. So what reward do you think Jesus is talking about?

_____

_____

• What does it mean to be "sons of the Most High?"

_____

_____

• Why do you think God is kind to the ungrateful and wicked?

_____

_____

• Do you think it's difficult for God to show us mercy? Why or why not?

_____

_____

Leader Instructions

After groups have finished the "The Good, the Bad, and the Ugly—How to Handle Conflict" page, process the experience with questions such as:

- How did this experience help you better understand Jesus' advice?

- In your own words, how would you sum up Jesus' advice?

Apply It

Find a partner, and read the following Scriptures together. After reading the Scriptures, tell your partner which passage is the most meaningful to you right now and why.

- Proverbs 15:1
- Matthew 18:21-22
- Luke 23:34
- Ephesians 4:26

After you've shared your thoughts, turn to the "Conflict Resolution Prayer" (p. 20) and follow the instructions. When you've both completed the prayer, take turns praying aloud for each other. Ask God to give your partner the strength and courage to follow Christ's example in handling conflict.

Extension Idea

You might want to expand Section 1 of the "The Good, the Bad, and the Ugly—How to Handle Conflict" activity by bringing in props for your actors, having groups present their pantomimes for one another, or videotaping the performances.

Tell Me More...

"The human beings around us are often the bottles that hold our medicine, but it is our Father's hand of love that pours out the medicine, and compels us to drink it. The human bottle is the 'second cause' of our trial; but it has no real agency in it, for the medicine that these human 'bottles' hold is prescribed for us and given to us by the Great Physician of our souls, who is seeking thereby to heal all our spiritual diseases.

"For instance, I know of no better medicine to cure the disease of irritability than to be compelled to live with a human 'bottle' of sensitiveness whom we are bound to consider and yield to."

(Hannah Whitall Smith, *The Christian's Secret of a Happy Life*)

Conflict Resolution Prayer

Read the prayer below, and thoughtfully fill in the blanks. You won't have to share what you write with anyone.

Dear God,

Thank you for giving me your example of how to handle conflicts in my life.

Please help me the next time I get angry with

_____. Help me to treat him or her as you would.

Please forgive me for _____. Help me listen to your advice and remember it the next time I

_____.

And please give me the courage to love my enemies, not just the people who love me. Help me love _____ and _____.

The situation in which I'm most afraid I won't be able to follow your advice is

_____. Please be with me then.

Lord, thank you for loving me and forgiving me. Help me show this same love and forgiveness to others.

Signed,

_____

Live It

Take some time this week to do the following experiment. First, reread Luke 6:27-36.

This week as you read your local paper, jot down the facts of several stories that involve conflict. Rewrite the endings of the stories, imagining that the people involved had followed Jesus' advice. (This is also a fun exercise to do with advice columns such as "Dear Abby.")

_____

_____

_____

_____

_____

_____

_____

_____

_____

_____

_____

_____

_____

Think about these questions:

- How do you think Jesus feels when he sees the people he died for arguing and fighting with one another?
- How would society be different if more people followed Christ's example?
- How would your life be different?

Tell Me More...

"How far you go in life depends on your being tender with the young, compassionate with the aged, sympathetic with the striving, and tolerant of the weak and the strong—because someday you will have been all of those."

—George Washington Carver

Learning to Forgive

✪ **Because God has forgiven us, we can forgive others.**

Supplies: You'll need Bibles, pencils or pens, and a cassette player and a cassette tape of soft instrumental music (optional).

Preparation: On a table, set out Bibles and pencils or pens to use during the study.

Leader Instructions

Begin by having students read the "Read About It" section and respond in the "Write About It" section.

Read About It

An architect received the commission of his life: designing the high altar of a new cathedral.

The architect soon discovered everyone had a suggestion, so he listened patiently. Then he closed his study door to work alone.

The day arrived when the architect showed his design to an expectant crowd. As the design was unveiled, the crowd gasped. There was no altar at all! The floor at the front of the cathedral was level and open beneath a simple wooden cross.

"Explain this…this…*sacrilege!*" blustered the bishop. "What does this *blasphemy* say about our holy Lord?"

The architect paused a long moment. "At the foot of the cross there's room for everyone," he finally said, pointing to the large, open area. "And the ground is level."

The architect was immediately fired.

Write About It

- What do you think the architect was trying to say through his design? Do you agree or disagree with his statement? Explain.

_____

_____

- Do you agree with the idea behind the architect's design? Why or why not?

_____

_____

- Do you think anyone is beyond God's forgiveness through Jesus? If so, who do you think might fit into this category? Why?

_____

_____

- How forgiving are you? Rank yourself as compared to other people (check one):

Much more forgiving than others   _____

Somewhat more forgiving than others   _____

About the same as others   _____

Less forgiving than most others   _____

Much less forgiving than most others   _____

- Now rank how forgiving you are compared to Jesus (check one):

Much more forgiving than Jesus   _____

Somewhat more forgiving than Jesus   _____

About the same as Jesus   _____

Less forgiving than Jesus   _____

Much less forgiving than Jesus   _____

- What does your ranking compared to Jesus' ranking tell you about yourself?

_____

_____

_____

Experience It

Form a trio with two other people. You'll be assigned a Forgiveness Profile Card to consider.

Leader Instructions

After trios have formed, assign each trio one of the Forgiveness Profile Cards to read (it's OK if more than one trio reads the same card).

If you feel it's necessary, you may want to offer a brief synopsis of Judas' betrayal of Jesus (Forgiveness Profile Card 1) or a brief synopsis of the Nazi regime (Forgiveness Profile Card 2).

In your trio, read Section 1 of your card and discuss the questions listed. Answer the "Going Deeper" questions individually, and share the answers with your trio if you feel comfortable doing so.

Leader Instructions

Allow six minutes for discussion of Section 1 of the Forgiveness Profile Cards. When it's time to wrap up the discussion, announce two- and one-minute warnings.

Then read and discuss Section 2.

Leader Instructions

Allow six minutes for discussion of Section 2, again announcing two- and one-minute warnings.

Report to the larger group any insights or significant comments made by someone in your trio.

Forgiveness Profile Card 1

Section 1

Did he do it for the money? Did he do it because he was angry that Jesus didn't raise an army and fight the Romans? We really don't know why he did it...but we are sure that Judas secretly negotiated with the Jewish political leaders to turn Jesus over to them. We're sure that he took money for his part in the plot. And we're sure that he betrayed Jesus with a kiss of friendship.

Betrayal...hypocrisy...accomplice to murder...there's a lot to hold against Judas. Discuss these questions in your trio:

- Which of Judas' crimes do you think was the worst? Why?
- What do you think motivated Judas to do what he did? Does his motivation excuse his actions? Why or why not?
- Do you believe Jesus forgave Judas? Why or why not?

Going Deeper

(Share your answers only if you're comfortable doing so.)

- Have you ever been guilty of claiming to love Jesus but acting in a way that was inconsistent with that claim? Explain.
- Have you ever been guilty of betraying others? If so, how?

Section 2

We tend to judge Judas harshly. We find it difficult to believe he could betray God's Son. Yet none of the disciples got through that night without betraying Jesus in word (denying Jesus) or deed (simply vanishing into the night to hide).

We've betrayed Jesus too. We've sinned by denying him with our words or deeds. We've run away from opportunities to openly identify with Jesus. We have no high moral ground on which to stand when we condemn Judas. If God forgives us, how can we deny forgiveness to Judas?

Discuss these questions:

- Do you agree with what's written above? Why or why not?
- If what's written above is true, what does it say about Jesus? about you? about your relationship with Jesus?

Forgiveness Profile Card 2

Section 1

Her name was Corrie ten Boom, and for the crime of sheltering Jews, she and her sister were imprisoned in the Nazis' Ravensbruck concentration camp. Her sister died in the camp, and Corrie nearly perished.

Years later, a camp guard who had brutalized both Corrie and her sister heard her speak at a church in Munich. He didn't recognize Corrie, but he reached out his hand, asking for her forgiveness. Corrie froze. She had never expected to see the guard again—especially not in church.

Corrie said a quick prayer, asking God to give her the strength to forgive. Then she reached out her hand to the man.

Nazis. The very name conjures up images of jackbooted evil. We marvel at how Hitler and his followers could have murdered millions, looted nations, and launched a war that consumed a generation. There's a lot to hold against Nazis like the guard who stretched out a hand to Corrie ten Boom.

Discuss these questions in your trio:

- What crime of the Nazi regime do you think was the worst? Explain.
- What do you think motivated the Nazis? Does any motivation excuse their actions? Why or why not?
- Do you believe Jesus could forgive Hitler? Could he forgive a Nazi guard at Ravensbruck? Why or why not?

Going Deeper

(Share your answers only if you're comfortable doing so.)

- The Nazis abused power. Have you abused power? If so, how?
- The Nazis abused people. Have you abused people? If so, how?

Section 2

We tend to judge the Nazis harshly, believing they were so evil that they can't possibly be anything like us. Yet we, too, have misused power, treated others cruelly, and acted out of vengeance or anger. We have no high moral ground on which to stand while tossing stones at the Nazis. If God forgives us, how can we deny forgiveness to the Nazis?

Discuss these questions:

- Do you agree with what's written above? Why or why not?
- If what's written above is true, what does it say about Jesus? about you? about your relationship with Jesus?

Now stand, stretch, and consider yourself drafted into the "instant drama troupe." Volunteer for one of the following roles: the king, the king's servant, the servant's buddy, the jailer, the tattletale servants, or sound effects.

Leader Instructions

Read aloud Matthew 18:21-22 as an introduction to the production. Then read aloud verses 23-35. Pause where appropriate to allow actors to move or for sound effects people to provide an appropriate soundtrack.

As the leader reads the passage aloud, move or create sound effects where your part is indicated.

Now give yourselves a round of applause, and then pair up with someone new and discuss these questions:

Extension Idea

Videotape the drama segment of the session, and play it back for the group's enjoyment.

- Which character in this production do you think was most pleasing to God? Why?
- Which character reminds you of yourself? Why?
- On your own, write five words that describe how you feel about Jesus' comment about forgiving others and how our heavenly Father will treat us: _____, _____, _____, _____, _____.
  Share what you wrote with your partner.

Apply It

Leader Instructions

Place a chair in front of the room. If possible, play soft instrumental music as students grapple with the questions in this section.

We all have people in our lives who we need to forgive—people who have hurt us, disappointed us, or betrayed our trust.

Write the name of a person you need to forgive on this line:

_____

Now mentally place the person in the empty chair in front of you. As you examine the following Scripture passages, consider how they apply to you and the person you've placed in this chair.

Matthew 6:12

_____

_____

Mark 11:25

_____

_____

Luke 6:37

_____

_____

Colossians 3:13

_____

_____

Find a partner. Sit with this person, knee to knee. Together, ask God for the grace to welcome to the foot of the cross the people whose names you wrote. Thank God for the forgiveness he's offered to you. Thank God for the forgiveness he's offered to everyone, including the people you identified as needing your forgiveness. Ask God for the ability to forgive.

Live It

We hate apologizing, and we'll often go to great lengths to avoid having to admit we're wrong.

By definition, being wrong is part of the human condition. Only Jesus was ever completely blameless, and unless you claim divinity you've got something to apologize for.

Who is someone you've offended or wronged? Make contact with that person to ask forgiveness for your offense.

1. Write the name here: _____

2. When will you make the call? Write the day and time here:

_____

3. Ask God for strength and wisdom to follow through. God has a lot of experience in the forgiveness department.

Tell Me More...

Jesus did more than just talk about forgiveness—he _embodied_ it. Consider the impact Jesus had on the people he met. Read Luke 5:8 to see how Peter responded to Jesus, and then read John 4:29 to discover how a Samaritan woman recognized Jesus as more than simply a teacher.

Real Friendship

God shows us how to be good friends to one another.

Supplies: You'll need Bibles, pencils or pens, poster board, scissors, markers, masking tape, index cards, and several long lengths of lightweight rope.

Preparation: On a table, set out the supplies to use during the study.

Leader Instructions

Begin by having students each read the "Read About It" section and respond in the "Write About It" section.

Read About It

Two Travelers were on the road together, when a Bear suddenly appeared on the scene. Before he observed them, one made for a tree at the side of the road, and climbed up into the branches and hid there. The other was not so nimble as his companion; and, as he could not escape, he threw himself on the ground and pretended to be dead. The Bear came up and sniffed all around him, but he kept perfectly still and held his breath; for they say that a bear will not touch a dead body. The Bear took him for a corpse, and went away. When the coast was clear, the Traveler in the tree came down, and asked the other what it was the Bear had whispered to him when he put his mouth to his ear. The other replied, "He told me never again to travel with a friend who deserts you at the first sign of danger."

(Aesop, *The Book of Virtues*)

Write About It

• Describe a time you were "left in the dust" by a friend. How did you feel?

_____

_____

_____

_____

- Describe a time you helped a friend in danger.

_____

_____

_____

_____

- On a scale from one to ten (ten is high), rate your ability to be a good friend. Tell why you rated yourself as you did.

_____

_____

_____

Experience It

Leader Instructions

Have students form four groups, and point out the supply table you've prepared before the study.

In your group, follow the instructions on the "Real-Life Friendships" page (p. 30). Use the supplies on the supply table as needed.

Tell Me More...

The Greek word for friendship, "philia," involves the idea of loving as well as being loved. *Philia* is the perfect example of friendship being a two-way street. We're supposed to rely on friendship from our friends as well as being someone they can expect friendship from.

Extension Idea

For the first section of "Real-Life Friendships," consider having groups act out the scenarios. After each group has acted out its scene, gather together as one large group and discuss the corresponding questions.

Real-Life Friendships
Section 1

As a group, read Proverbs 17:17 three times so you know it well. Then discuss the following questions, and write the answers in the space provided.

• What type of adversity do you think this verse is speaking of?

_____

_____

• What does it mean to be a brother born for adversity?

_____

_____

• How would you state the opposite of this verse?

_____

_____

To get a handle on what it might mean to be a brother born for adversity, read through the situations and answer the questions in the spaces provided:

You've been friends with Jenny for a long time. Just now she walked up to you, told you off, and ran into her third-period classroom.

• Should you approach Jenny right now? If so, what's the best way to approach her?

_____

_____

• According to Proverbs, what might be the correct course of action?

_____

_____

You decide to go talk to Jenny. When you get to her, she's huddled in the corner sobbing uncontrollably. She explains that she's had a big fight with another of your best friends.

• How should you approach this situation, knowing that two people you care about are having a serious conflict?

_____

_____

• How can you be a brother born for adversity for your two friends at the same time?

_____

_____

Just as you're talking to Jenny, Sheila (the friend Jenny's had the big fight with) walks into the room. She looks as if she's ready for another brawl.

• What are the first three things you need to do or say?

_____

_____

• How can you love your two friends through this situation?

_____

_____

• How do you think Jesus would handle this situation?

_____

_____

Section 2

Read the following passages. As a group, discuss the corresponding questions and write your answers in the space provided.

• Read 1 Samuel 20:1-11. What friendship principles do you notice in this passage?

_____

_____

• Read 1 Samuel 20:12-23. What friendship principles do you notice in this passage?

_____

_____

• Read 1 Samuel 20:24-34. What friendship principles do you notice in this passage?

_____

_____

• Read 1 Samuel 20:35-42. What friendship principles do you notice in this passage?

_____

_____

Look over the list of principles you've created from reading the passages above. On your own, choose one principle and use the poster board and other supplies to create a symbol of that principle. Once group members have created their symbols, discuss what you've created. Discuss these questions in your group:

• What did you learn about friendship from the passages and the symbols?

• What did you learn about God's place in friendship from the passages and the symbols?

• How can you be a friend to someone who is involved in sinful behaviors (for example, doing drugs or having premarital sex)?

God has not only encouraged us to be good friends, he's asked us to be the best friends that we can be. Read John 15:14-15. Since God has been our best friend, he wants us to model that and be a good friend to other people.

• How has God proven his friendship to you?

• As a friend, what are some qualities that you need to develop?

Section 3

Read Ecclesiastes 4:9-12. As a group, discuss the following questions and write the answers in the space provided:

- This passage begins by mentioning two people but ends by using an analogy of three strands. Who might the third strand represent? Explain.

_____

_____

_____

- What impact does God have on our friendships?

_____

_____

_____

- How can we make sure that the "third strand" in our friendships is a strong one?

_____

_____

_____

Divide your group into two separate teams. Get a length of rope and some masking tape from the supply table. Place a piece of tape in the middle of the rope, and put tape in two places, approximately three feet apart, on the floor. Place the center of the rope halfway between the two pieces of tape on the floor. Using the rope, organize a group tug of war. The team who gets pulled over the line must brainstorm ways to strengthen friendships. Do this several times. As you brainstorm, use the index cards and write one idea on each card. Then hang each card somewhere on the rope. You'll end up with your tug-of-war rope filled with ways to strengthen friendships. When you've finished, discuss these questions in your group and write the answers in the space provided:

- In this game, how is needing strong rope like needing to have a strong friendship?

_____

_____

_____

- How might you work to strengthen a friendship when a friend has turned against you?

_____

_____

_____

- How can you tell whether a friendship is strong?

_____

_____

_____

Leader Instructions

After groups have finished the "Real-Life Friendships" page, process the experience using questions such as these:

- Which Scripture did you relate to the most? Explain.
- After completing this experience, again rate yourself on your ability to be a good friend. On a scale from one to ten (ten is high), what is your ability to be a good friend?
- Has your ability to be a good friend changed as a result of this experience? Explain.

Apply It

Find a partner. Reread the story at the beginning of today's study. Decide which person best describes you—the person on the ground or the person in the tree. Tell your partner about a time you acted as one of the people in the story did.

Look at the "Making Friendship Work" picture below, and write on the bear some things that might hurt your friendships. Next, beside the person sitting on the ground, write some ways you might approach a friend whom you've hurt. Finally, next to the person sitting in the tree, write some ways to build a healthy friendship. When you've recorded your responses, share with your partner what you've written.

Making Friendship Work

Think of a commitment you'd like to make regarding your friendships and that you will follow through on during the coming week. This might be committing to repair a hurting friendship or to reach out to someone who needs a friend. Base your commitment on the biblical principles you have learned about today. Write your commitment here: _____

_____

Share your commitment with your partner, and then pray aloud for each other, asking God to help you follow his example of friendship in your own friendships.

Live It

Take the "Apply It" section one step further by doing the following research study:

1. When you go shopping, look for people who are shopping with their friends. Answer the following questions:

• How do they treat each other?

_____

_____

_____

• Do they seem to enjoy being together? How can you tell?

_____

_____

_____

2. As you watch television, answer the following questions:

• How does television portray friendships?

_____

_____

_____

• Is God included in any of the friendships you view? In what way?

_____

_____

_____

3. While at church, notice people greeting each other who might be friends and then answer the following questions:

• Do people's friendships seem more formal at church? Explain.

_____

_____

_____

• Do friendships appear to be strengthened through attending church? Explain.

_____

_____

_____

• How does your pastor relate to people who might be his friends?

_____

_____

_____

Authorities: Awful or Awesome?

 **Human authority is given by God.**

Supplies: You'll need Bibles and pencils or pens.

Preparation: On a table, set out the supplies to use during the study.

Leader Instructions

Begin by having students each read the "Read About It" section and respond in the "Write About It" section.

Read About It

Why is authority important? Consider these guidelines adapted from an article published many years ago by the United States Chamber of Commerce:

How to Train Your Child to Be a Delinquent

1. When your child is still an infant, give her everything she wants. This way she'll think the world owes her a living when she grows up.

2. When he picks up swearing and dirty jokes, laugh at him and encourage him. As he grows up, he'll pick up "cuter" phrases that will floor you.

3. Never give her any spiritual training. Wait until she's twenty-one, and let her decide for herself.

4. Avoid using the word *wrong*. It will give your child a guilt complex. You can condition him to believe later, when he is arrested for stealing a car, that society is against him and that he is being persecuted.

5. Pick up after her—her books, shoes, and clothes. Do everything for her so she will be experienced in throwing all responsibility onto others.

6. Let him read all printed matter he can get his hands on. Never think of monitoring TV programs, movies, or Internet exploration. Sterilize the silverware, but let him feast his mind on garbage.

7. Take her side against neighbors, teachers, and policemen. They're all against her.

(adapted from Charles Swindoll, *The Quest for Character*)

Write About It

• What do the guidelines you just read tell you about why your parents do some of the things they do?

_____

_____

_____

• What things sometimes bug you about your parents and other authorities?

_____

_____

_____

• Read Proverbs 22:6. How does this verse relate to the guidelines you read earlier?

_____

_____

_____

Experience It

Leader Instructions

Have students form groups of four or five.

In your group, follow the instructions in Section 1 of the "Why Are Authorities Important?" page (p. 39).

Leader Instructions

When groups have finished Section 1, have them present their stories. Then as a whole group, discuss these questions:

- *Why does God want us to obey our parents?*
- *What insights has this activity given you about parental authority?*
- *Where does parental authority come from? Why do you think this is?*

In your group, follow the instructions for Section 2 on the "Why Are Authorities Important?" page.

Extension Idea

For Section 1, you might want to use a camcorder to video-tape the stories and then play them back on a VCR and TV.

For Section 2, consider providing students with simple musical instruments to accompany the songs. Or have groups use tape recorders to record their songs before the presentations.

Leader Instructions

When groups have finished Section 2, have them present their songs. Then as a whole group, discuss these questions:

- Who gives human leaders their authority? Why do you think this is?
- As Christians, what negative impact could we have by being disobedient to our country's laws and authorities?
- What positive impact could we have through obedience?
- Read Acts 5:27-29. Under what circumstances might God want us to disobey a human authority?
- How can we decide when we should obey and when we should disobey?

Tell Me More...

"There are no degrees of obedience—we either obey, or disobey. When we implicitly obey the Scriptures, Jesus can shape our lives and make us the people we ought to be. For example, the Bible says, 'Wives, submit to your husbands, as is fitting in the Lord. Husbands, love your wives and do not be harsh with them. Children, obey your parents in everything, for this pleases the Lord. Fathers, do not embitter your children, or they will become discouraged' (Colossians 3:18-21). If we, as Christians, could take that message, meditate on it, and apply it to our lives, wouldn't that enable the Christian home to bring great glory to God? At the rate Christian homes are breaking up today, we need God's divine intervention. May God help us to be obedient Christians."

(Charles Riggs, *Learning to Walk With God*)

Why Are Authorities Important?

Section 1: In the News

Your group is a news team compiling a report about someone who's been in the news. Use the following statements to help you complete your report.

Jason Edwards, 23, has been convicted of a string of burglaries and sentenced to six years in prison.

Read Ephesians 6:1-3, and work with your group to write the rest of Jason's story. Base your story on how Jason's life might have led to his prison sentence, following the principles in the passage. Have fun with the story, but be sure to get across the point of the passage.

During Jason's early childhood...

_____

_____

Jason's problems began when he...

_____

_____

As a teenager, Jason...

_____

_____

Jason's parents...

_____

_____

When confronted with his wrongdoing by the judge, Jason...

_____

_____

Things could have been so different if Jason had...

_____

_____

Section 2: The Authority-Driven Hillbillies

Read 1 Peter 2:13-17, and then work together with other group members to write a song about someone who follows the guidelines of this passage. Use the tune from *The Beverly Hillbillies* theme song or another familiar song. Have fun with this, but be sure to get across the message of the Bible passage.

_____

_____

_____

_____

_____

_____

_____

_____

Apply It

On your own, brainstorm a bunch of things your parents tell you to do or not to do that bug you:

_____

_____

_____

Leader Instructions

Have students read their responses to you, and compile a list on a sheet of newsprint or a chalkboard.

Have students form new groups of four or five, and assign each group at least three or four things from the list you compiled.

Put yourself in your parents' place. Suggest reasons your parents might have for asking you to do or not to do the things your group has been assigned. Fill in each numbered section below with one parent command and your group's suggested reason for that command. Keep in mind the Scriptures you examined earlier.

1. It really bugs me when my parents tell me...

_____

_____

But we think they do it because...

_____

_____

2. It really bugs me when my parents tell me...

_____

_____

But we think they do it because...

_____

_____

3. It really bugs me when my parents tell me...

_____

_____

But we think they do it because...

_____

_____

4. It really bugs me when my parents tell me...

_____

_____

But we think they do it because...

_____

_____

_____

Leader Instructions ✏️

When groups have finished, have them report their results to the whole class.

Write your answers to these questions on your own:

• Do you think your parents would agree with your group's assessment of their motives? Why or why not?

_____

_____

_____

_____

Tell Me More...

"To submit to rulers and authorities does not mean blind obedience... God's authority stands behind every government, right or wrong, but it also stands 'over' every human authority, not allowing evil to go unchecked forever.

"If government parallels God's law, then Christians are right to obey it. However, if a human law runs counter to God's principles, then it is not wrong to disobey. Even while resisting in those areas where government oversteps its bounds...though, Christians must still recognize the authority of government in its other functions. In this way, Christians can obey God with a clear conscience."

(Quest Study Bible)

• Why would God give your parents the authority they have?

_____

_____

_____

• How is the authority God has given to other leaders the same as the authority he has given to your parents? How is it different?

_____

_____

_____

Now here are the big questions:

• How should you treat your parents, knowing what we've discussed in this study?

_____

_____

_____

_____

• How should you respond to other authorities, knowing what we've discussed in this study?

_____

_____

_____

Find a partner, and share your answers with him or her. Then think about how you treat your parents. Choose one area you'll commit to working on, and share it with your partner. Then pray together, asking God to help you fulfill your commitments.

Tell Me More...

"When I was a boy of fourteen, my father was so ignorant I could hardly stand to have him around. But when I got to be twenty-one, I was astonished at how much he had learned in seven years."

—Mark Twain

Live It

• Think about things you do that show respect to your parents' authority. Write three here:

_____

_____

_____

• Think about three things you do that show disrespect toward your parents' authority. Write them here:

_____

_____

_____

_____

• Read Proverbs 23:22-25. Use the passage to help you describe the attitude you'll determine to have toward your parents and how your parents will see that attitude in your actions.

_____

_____

_____

_____

Dating 101

 The Bible gives us solid guidelines for good dating relationships.

Supplies: You'll need Bibles and pens or pencils.

Preparation: On a table, set out the supplies to use during the study.

Leader Instructions

Begin by having students each read the "Read About It" section and respond in the "Write About It" section.

Read About It

Love or Infatuation?

Infatuation is instant desire. It is one set of glands calling to another. Love is friendship that has caught fire. It takes root and grows—one day at a time.

Infatuation is marked by a feeling of insecurity.

You are excited and eager but not genuinely happy. There are nagging doubts, unanswered questions, little bits and pieces about your beloved that you would just as soon not examine too closely. It might spoil the dream.

Love is quiet understanding and the mature acceptance of imperfection. It is real. It gives you strength and grows beyond you—to bolster your beloved. You are warmed by his presence, even when he is away. Miles do not separate you. You want him nearer. But near or far, you know he is yours and you can wait.

Infatuation says, "We must get married right away. I can't risk losing him."

Love says, "Be patient. Don't panic. Plan your future with confidence."

Infatuation lacks confidence. When he's away, you wonder if he's cheating. Sometimes you check.

Love means trust. You are calm, secure and unthreatened. He feels that trust, and it makes him even more trustworthy.

...Infatuation might lead you to do things you'll regret later, but love never will.

Love is an upper. It makes you look up. It makes you think up. It makes you a better person than you were before.

(Ann Landers, *Wake Up and Smell the Coffee!*)

Write About It

- Do you agree with these definitions of love and infatuation? Why or why not?

_____

_____

_____

- Which do you think is more common in your dating relationships—love or infatuation? Explain.

_____

_____

_____

- Why do people date? What is the ultimate purpose of dating?

_____

_____

_____

- What would your perfect date be like?

_____

_____

_____

- Read Genesis 2:18. What do you think this verse means? How does it apply in today's society?

_____

_____

_____

Experience It

Leader Instructions

For the first part of this activity, have the girls form one group and the guys form another group. Point out the supply table you've prepared for the study.

In your group, follow the instructions in Part 1 of "The Dating Game" page (p. 47).

Leader Instructions

While groups work, place three chairs side by side in the center of the room, all facing in one direction. Place another chair behind these three chairs, facing away from them.

In your group, follow the instructions in Part 2 of "The Dating Game" page.

Leader Instructions

Act as the "emcee" during Part 2, keeping things running smoothly. Encourage students to ham it up by mimicking the TV show (within reason!).

Extension Idea

To make "The Dating Game" more fun, hang a curtain or sheet between the single chair and the other three chairs. Not only will the barrier allow groups to guess who's asking and answering the questions, but it may also provide enough anonymity to eliminate any shyness during the activity.

In your group, follow the instructions in Parts 3 and 4 of "The Dating Game" page.

Tell Me More...

Here's a humorous look at the search for an ideal mate:

How to Develop a Psychological Profile of Your Ideal Mate

Choose the phrase that you feel best completes the sentences below:

Wealth

The person I wish to have for a mate should be able to afford:

1. Scotland.
2. Occasional dinners out.
3. Underwear.

Sensitivity

The person I wish to have for a mate should be sensitive enough to:

1. Instantly be aware of my every mood.
2. Swerve to avoid driving over pedestrians.
3. Not deliberately back up and run over pedestrians a second time.

Personal Appearance

The person I wish to have for a mate should be attractive enough to:

1. Be a movie star.
2. Be a movie star's accountant.
3. Be a movie star's accountant's intestinal parasite.

Intelligence

The person I wish to have for a mate should be smart enough to:

1. Discuss great works of literature.
2. Hold great works of literature right side up.
3. Differentiate between great works of literature and food.

(Dave Barry, *Dave Barry's Guide to Life*)

The Dating Game

Part 1

As a group, discuss and write answers to the following questions. It's OK if you write more than one answer to each question—just make sure everyone in your group joins in the discussion.

• What would your dream date look like?

_____

• Where would you go on a perfect date?

_____

• What three qualities would be most important in a dream date?

_____

Part 2

Girls, choose one person from your group to ask the following questions. Guys, choose three volunteers from your group to answer the questions. Sit in the appropriate chairs. Guys, try to answer these questions in the way you think the girls answered them in Part 1. Then switch roles, and play the game again. Here are "The Dating Game" questions:

• Dream Date, what do you look like?
• Dream Date, where would we go on our first date?
• Dream Date, what three qualities do you have that I would most appreciate?

Part 3

As a group, discuss and write answers to the following questions. It's OK if you write more than one answer to each question—just make sure everyone in your group joins in the discussion.

• How did the other group's answers compare with your answers from Part 1?

_____

• Based on this activity, do you think guys and girls have the same expectations about dating? Explain.

_____

_____

• Do you think it's possible for guys and girls to agree on what constitutes a good date? Why or why not?

_____

_____

Part 4

In your group, read Philippians 2:1-4; 4:8-9. Then discuss and write answers to the following questions:

• What qualities do these passages say are important?

_____

• How do the qualities mentioned in these passages differ from the ones you listed in Part 1? in Part 2?

_____

• How do you think God would want you to answer the questions in Part 1?

_____

Apply It

Find a partner of the opposite sex. Decide which of you will read first. Have that person read aloud again Philippians 2:1-4, and then have the other person read aloud again Philippians 4:8-9.

Leader Instructions

If you don't have equal numbers of guys and girls, it's OK to have a few trios.

Next, turn to the "This Is Your Life" page (p. 49). Read the scenarios, and write your answers based on your gender. For example, if you're a guy, answer from Joe's perspective. If you're a girl, answer from Jane's perspective. Try to incorporate the advice of the passages you've just read.

Then read your answers to your partner, and discuss what was similar or different in your perspectives. Do you agree with the way your partner answered? Why or why not?

Next, discuss these questions with your partner:

• How realistic do you think it is to live out biblical characteristics in your dating relationships?
• What might keep you from following the Bible's advice?
• Do you see any danger in always putting someone else first, especially when it comes to dating? Explain.

This Is Your Life

Scenario 1

Joe and Jane have been dating for several months. There's a Valentine's Day dance coming up at school, and Jane has already bought a new dress for the occasion. But Joe's older brother is coming home from the Army that weekend. What should Jane and Joe say to each other?

_____

_____

_____

_____

Scenario 2

Jane and Joe are out on their first date, with a group of friends. After the movie, everybody decides to go back to Gene's house because his parents are out of town. Jane and Joe know there will probably be drinking at Gene's house, but neither of them wants to seem like a nerd. What should they say to each other?

_____

_____

_____

Scenario 3

Jane and Joe have been together for almost a year. They believe they're truly in love, and they don't know whether they really need to wait until they're married to have sex. What should they say to each other?

_____

_____

_____

_____

Now on your own, write a letter to God, thanking him for claiming you and asking him to keep your dating relationships within his guidelines. For example, you might say, "Please make me the kind of date who…" and "Please let me date someone who…" As a closing prayer, read your letter to your partner.

Live It

Interview several married couples, and ask them the following questions:

• What keeps your marriage strong?
• How has your relationship changed from the way it was when you were dating?
• How did you know you were in love?

At school, listen to the casual remarks people make about dating and relationships. Then ask yourself these questions:

• How well do these remarks reflect the biblical values I've read about?
• What can I learn from these remarks?

Tell Me More…

"Remember O. Henry's 'The Gift of the Magi'? It is Christmas, and a poor but loving couple have no money to buy each other any gifts. So, she cuts her beautiful long hair and sells it to a wig maker in order to buy [her husband] a gold chain for his family heirloom gold watch. As it turns out, he has sold his gold watch to buy her a beautiful comb to decorate her hair. If you…don't experience mutual loving sacrifice like this while you're courting…forget it!"

(Dr. Laura Schlessinger, *Ten Stupid Things Men Do to Mess Up Their Lives*)

Never Alone

 God's constant presence gives us comfort and hope in lonely times.

Supplies: You'll need Bibles, pens or pencils, modeling clay, small cardboard squares, pieces of cloth (or paper) slightly bigger than the cardboard, craft sticks, and markers.

Preparation: On a table, set out the supplies to use during the study.

Leader Instructions

Begin by having students each read the "Read About It" section and respond in the "Write About It" section.

Read About It

I've never felt so lonely as I did the year my family fell apart.

It was an evening I'll never forget. The thunderstorm outside woke me up, but it was the loud sobbing that kept me awake. I ran downstairs and found my dad staring blankly at the TV and my mom with her face pressed into the couch cushions, crying uncontrollably. "You know I love you, don't you, son?" my dad asked. "I'm leaving tomorrow morning—I'll be living across town for awhile. I think your mom will eventually understand."

I was losing my dad. And that was just the beginning.

Mom was never quite the same. Before long, she tried to kill herself several times. Her desire to die basically left my brother and I to raise ourselves. Not only had I lost my dad, I was losing my mom as well.

Then came the final blow—my brother announced he was gay. All of the "friends" he had over for the night, were, well, you know. He was dating them. My dad was gone. My mom was doing what she could to end her life. And my brother left to fulfill his dreams and hide his shame.

I was left alone. And I felt very lonely. It felt as if everyone I'd ever loved had decided that other things were more important than I was.

And then I met God. It wasn't through a Christian TV show or a really great book. I met him through one person who took the time to show me how important I was. Through this person, God showed me that, to him, I mattered more than anything, no matter what my family did.

For the first time, I felt as if I belonged to someone. And I felt that I was loved more than I would ever understand. More than anything, God helped me see that when I'm lonely, he's waiting to throw his arms around me and show me how much I matter to him.

Write About It

• What's the difference between being alone and being lonely?

_____

_____

_____

_____

• When have you felt lonely?

_____

_____

_____

_____

• Read Psalm 22:12-18. Is this an accurate view of how you feel when you're lonely? What are some other feelings you have when you're lonely?

_____

_____

_____

_____

• What has given you comfort when you've felt lonely?

_____

_____

_____

_____

Experience It

Leader Instructions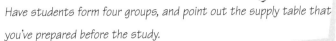

Have students form four groups, and point out the supply table that you've prepared before the study.

In your group, follow the instructions on the "Knowing God's Presence" page (p. 54). Use the supplies on the supply table as needed.

Leader Instructions

In Section 1, the question "Why do you think God allows us to feel lonely?" might open a can of worms with the group. If tough questions arise, consider the following answers:

- *Sometimes, God might allow us to feel lonely to bring us to a place of dependence on him. While God doesn't like the emotions that are associated with it, loneliness is one way to clear a path to him.*

- *Loneliness might be the result of sin. It isn't always the result of sin. Sin removes us from fellowship with God. If we are unrepentant for our sin, loneliness may result.*

Extension Idea

Consider modifying the activities in the first two sections by doing the following.

For Section 1, instead of using the modeling clay, have students freeze into a still-life portrait of someone dealing with loneliness. Gather everyone together, say "go," and have members freeze into their creations. Then, with teens still "frozen," have them share what their creations represent.

For Section 2, use a large sheet and have volunteers hold it over the still-life creations. Then have students share how it affects them to know God's covering of protection and presence is over them when they feel lonely.

Knowing God's Presence
Section 1

Read Psalm 22:19-21. As a group, discuss the following questions and write the answers in the spaces provided.

• What did this writer do when he felt lonely?

_____

• Describe the emotions this writer might have been feeling. Have you ever felt these types of emotions when you were lonely?

_____

_____

• What things cause you to feel lonely?

_____

• How do you handle loneliness?

_____

Using the modeling clay, work as a group to create a still-life model representing some of the causes of loneliness. You might want to create a still-life scene involving several people who deal with loneliness in different ways. Be sure to create your scene on a piece of cardboard, leaving room in the center of the cardboard. When you've finished, discuss these questions in your group and write the answers in the spaces provided:

• Why do you think God allows us to feel lonely?

_____

• What answers does the world offer when we're lonely?

_____

Section 2

Read Romans 8:38-39. As a group, discuss the following questions and write the answers in the spaces provided:

• This passage makes it clear that nothing can separate us from the love of God—not even loneliness. Rewrite this passage on your own to make the concept apply to you. Share what you've written with the rest of the group.

_____

• What steps can you take to help you remember the truth of this passage all the time—especially when you're lonely?

_____

• How does it make you feel to know that you can't escape God's love? Explain.

_____

In your group, take a few minutes to brainstorm the things God does to comfort us when we're lonely. When you've got a list, use the markers and write your favorite ideas on a fabric square.

When you've finished, tape one craft stick to each corner of the fabric. Then tape the sticks to the cardboard, creating a tent over your clay creations. Next, place another craft stick in the center of the cardboard to prop up the center of the tent. (See the picture at right.)

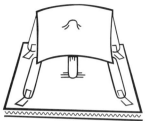

When you've finished, discuss these questions in your group and write the answers in the spaces provided.

• What are some barriers we put up that keep us from receiving God's comfort?

_____

• How does Romans 8:38-39 describe the covering that God provides for us?

_____

• God wants us to know he's always there. When we feel lonely, he wants to cover us with his comfort. Describe the way this makes you feel.

_____

Section 3

Read 1 Kings 19:1-18. As a group, discuss the following questions and write the answers in the spaces provided:

• What did Elijah do to experience God's presence?

_____

• How did Elijah know that the gentle whisper is God? Explain.

_____

• How do you think God's comfort for Elijah gave him strength to do what God asked next?

_____

As a group, gather in a circle around the clay structure and tent you've created. Spend the next few minutes talking about the ways God makes his presence, comfort, and encouragement known to us. For example, someone might say that God comforts us by giving us other people to talk to about our feelings. When you've finished, discuss these questions in your groups and write the answers in the spaces provided.

• How would you feel about God if you went through an experience like the one Elijah did?

_____

• Why do you think God doesn't comfort us by using big and powerful things like fire and earthquakes?

_____

• How does learning about God's desire to comfort us change your perspective on how to fill the void when you feel lonely? Explain.

_____

When you've finished answering the questions, gather together with the class and share your creation with everyone. Be sure to share the emotions that your clay sculptures portray, some of the ways God comforts us, and the ways he makes his comfort known to us.

Leader Instructions

After groups have finished the "Knowing God's Presence" page, process the experience using questions like the following:

- What are some insights you've gained from this experience?
- After completing this experience, what will you do differently when you feel lonely? Explain.
- What encouragement have you found in knowing that God never leaves you? Explain.

Apply It

Find a partner, and sit facing him or her. One at a time, share some of the promises you've heard today about God's presence when you feel lonely. You might say something like, "God is always ready to comfort me when I feel lonely" or "I have friends who will help me when I feel lonely." Divide the following passages with your partner: Genesis 28:15; Psalm 73:23; Matthew 10:29-31; and 1 Peter 3:12-13. As you read the Scriptures you've chosen, think about the promises God offers you in the face of loneliness.

When you've finished reading, draw a picture of an ear in the space below.

After you've drawn your picture, write some things you'll commit to do that will help you listen to God when you feel lonely. You might write things such as, "When I feel lonely, I'm going to stop, find a quiet place, and pray."

Once you've written your ideas, share them with each other and record your partner's ideas in your book as well. Then trade books with your partner, and write some of the ways you'll pray for your partner when he or she feels lonely. You might write that you'll pray that your partner is able to focus on God or will be able to find a friend when he or she is lonely.

After you've done this, read 1 John 4:17-18. Then spend some time praying for your partner. Be sure to thank God for his constant presence in your partner's life, and remember to share any concerns your partner might have concerning loneliness.

Live It

To get a deeper understanding of God's presence, start by answering the following questions:

• How would you respond to a friend who thinks that God must not love him or her because that friend hasn't felt God's comfort?

_____

_____

_____

• What are some ways you might advise your friend to listen and look for God's comfort? How might you use some of the Scripture passages in this study to help your friend understand God's comfort?

_____

_____

_____

• Do you know anyone who has dealt with serious loneliness but has worked through it? Write those people's names here:

_____

_____

_____

Find those people, and ask them to give you advice for the times you might feel lonely. If you can't think of anyone, or if you're really feeling lonely right now, consider talking to your parents or your pastor or youth worker. Talking about how you feel with someone who knows and loves you can help you deal with your loneliness and can help you realize that God is with you—right here, right now.

Tell Me More...

Trying to run away from loneliness is like trying to escape the chickenpox—it's pretty much impossible. But there are some things you can remember to help ease the loneliness you might feel.

- Loneliness does not come from God. He does not cause us to feel lonely to punish us. Nor does it make God happy when we feel lonely.

- The world offers things that will temporarily make you feel better, such as watching funny movies, expressing your feelings in unhealthy ways, or using drugs to forget how you feel. In the long run, these are empty solutions and shallow cures.

- Loneliness is often the result of a spiritual attack. Satan wants us to feel lonely. If he can get us to feel that God has deserted us, then he's doing what he does best. We have to make sure we don't give in to the attack and that we continue to follow God.

The cure for loneliness is like a mathematical equation. Loneliness + God's presence = comfort. At least that's the way it's supposed to work. The key, though, is knowing how to listen for God's voice. Sometimes it comes through a close friend. Other times it comes through reading his Word. It might come through a sermon you hear. And sometimes you might just be able to feel his arms around you. However God chooses to comfort you, you've got to be looking for it. God wants us to long for his comfort much like a thirsty person crawling across a desert longs for a large glass of water. When we feel lonely, God's comfort needs to be the one thing that we search for and the one thing that cures our hurts, emptiness, and hopelessness.

A Lifestyle of Love

 **We are to follow Christ's example of love.**

Supplies: You'll need Bibles, pens or pencils, a variety of assorted magazines, scissors, glue, construction paper or poster board, green and yellow highlighters, and two or three concordances (optional).

Preparation: On a table, set out the supplies to use during the study.

Leader Instructions

Begin by having students read the "Read About It" section and respond in the "Write About It" section.

Read About It

We hear a lot about love today—from friends, from movies, and from television. What we hear from these sources is often distorted. In the world's terms, love could be a warm feeling of infatuation for another person or an obsession with pizza. This ambiguity may lead people to do all sorts of immoral or hurtful things in the name of love.

But the Bible's depiction of love is clear. It speaks of passion, sacrifice, and concern for others. It tells of the fantastic love God has for us—and of what that love prompted him to do.

Write About It

• What things or people do you love? How do you know what you feel for these things or people is love?

_____

_____

• How do you know whether someone loves you?

_____

_____

_____

• Read Romans 5:6-8. How has God shown his love for you?

_____

_____

_____

• Write your own definition of love.

_____

_____

_____

Experience It

Leader Instructions 🖊

Have students form three groups, and assign a number from one to three to each group. Point out the supply table that you've prepared before the study.

In your group, follow the instructions on the "Perfect Example" page (p. 61).

Leader Instructions 🖊

In Section 1, encourage the group who is assigned "Eros" to use discretion in their choices.

When groups have finished their collages in Section 1, have them present their creations to the whole group.

For Section 2, assign 1 Corinthians 13:4-8 to one group and Romans 12:9-21 to the other two groups. When groups have finished filling out their charts, have them share their characteristics of love with the other groups. Make sure each group has all the characteristics of love written in its chart.

For Section 3, assign three of the provided Scripture passages to each group. When groups have finished filling in their charts, have them share their discoveries with the other groups. Be sure groups write all of the passages on their charts.

Perfect Example
Section 1

In English, we have only the word "love" to express love. That is, we may say we "love" Chinese food, our friends, our parents, and God. However, our feelings toward all of these things or people are probably different. The word "love" is required to encompass a great deal, and we often use "love" when we really mean "like." The English language only has one word for love, but there are several words for love in Greek, the language the New Testament was written in. Here are three of them:

1. *Philia* refers to the love between friends.

2. *Eros* is the love between lovers or "being in love."

3. *Agape* means unconditional love, just as God loves us.

In your group, create a visual display of the type of love that corresponds with your assigned number. Look through the magazines, and cut out pictures that display the type of love your group was assigned. Creatively display these pictures on your poster board or paper.

Section 2

As well as discussing types of love, the Bible often explains methods of expressing love. Paul, the author of much of the New Testament, developed many lists of ways to express love.

In your group, read your assigned Scripture (1 Corinthians 13:4-8 or Romans 12:9-21). Then in the first column of the chart below, write each characteristic of love that you discovered in your reading.

Characteristic of Love	Example	Me	Application

Discuss these questions:

• Which of these characteristics of love seem easy to follow?

_____

_____

_____

• Which characteristics of love seem difficult to follow or hard to understand?

_____

_____

_____

Section 3

Jesus Christ is the supreme example of love in action. The Gospels give us many wonderful examples of how Jesus displayed different characteristics of love.

With your group, investigate your assigned passages from the list below and write the Scripture reference or a brief description of each passage in the appropriate category on the "Example" column of the chart. Some of your passages will fit into more than one category, and some will be difficult to find a category for; just put them where you think they fit best.

• Matthew 4:23-25
• Matthew 8:1-4
• Matthew 11:28-30
• Luke 9:10-17
• Luke 19:1-7
• Luke 23:32-34
• John 4:1-16
• John 20:24-28
• John 21:15-19

If you have time, you may also locate other passages that display Jesus' love and include them on your chart (you may want to use a concordance).

Discuss the following questions in your group:

• Do you think Paul used his knowledge of Jesus' life to develop his lists of love?

• Do you think it was always easy for Jesus to love? Why?

• If you were in Jesus' position, in which situations would it have been difficult to love people?

• How has Jesus demonstrated his love to you?

Apply It

Get together with a partner, and share your answers from the "Write About It" section. Look at your definition of love. Do you think your definition has changed? With your partner, create a new definition of love and write it here:

_____

_____

_____

_____

Now look over the chart, and choose the characteristics of love you are strong in and the areas you are weak in. Share those characteristics with your partner. In the "Me" column of your chart, write the name of a person with whom you exercise each of your chosen characteristics of love. Highlight each of these names in yellow. Then write the name of a person with whom you need to exercise each characteristic of love, and highlight those names in green. With your partner, share specific ways you can exercise each characteristic of love with the people highlighted in green. In the "Application" column of your chart, write one way you will exercise each characteristic of love this week. Close by praying for each other, using this prayer starter: "Loving Savior, please help [partner's name] follow your example of love in his (or her) life this week by..."

Live It

The love Christ models sometimes differs from the love we read about, hear about, and watch in the popular media. The love the media portrays may be, in turn, erotic, passionate, passing, jealous, superficial, or genuine. This week, pay careful attention to the books you read, the songs you listen to, and the shows you watch. Each time you notice some type of love modeled, write the name of the book, song, TV show, or movie and the type of love you saw portrayed.

Name of show, song, or book	Name of show, song, or book	Name of show, song, or book
Type of Love	Type of Love	Type of Love

Extension Idea

Have students each think of a Christian adult who best exemplifies the love that Christ expressed. Encourage students to call the people they identified and interview them, using some of the following questions:

- Could you tell me a little about your life and how you came to know Christ?
- How do you love those that you don't want to love?
- Is it easy or difficult for you to love others?
- How do you define love?

• In the media, is love similar to or different from the type of love that Christ models? Explain.

_____

_____

_____

• What kinds of love does the media deem to be most important? least important?

_____

_____

_____

• How does the media shape your view of love?

_____

_____

_____

• How can you model Christ's love without allowing the world's views of love to interfere?

_____

_____

_____